Warning: This story contains a major spoiler from *Shadow's End* (book #9, released December 1st, 2015). If readers do not want to be spoiled, they should read the stories in order of their release dates.

This is a short story (15,000 words or 50 pages) intended for readers of the Elder Races who enjoy Liam Cuelebre as a character.

Reeling from a deep loss, the magical prince of the Wyr, Dragos and Pia's son Liam Cuelebre, turns inward and withdrawn as he struggles to come to terms with who he is, along with the challenges that lie before him.

Hoping to ease his heartache and offer comfort, a concerned Dragos and Pia offer him a gift, something he has desired for a long time. Liam's response has a ripple effect across all of New York. Soon miracles of all kinds start arriving just in time for Christmas, along with a visit from a mysterious person who gives Liam hope and a vision of his future.

Liam Takes Manhattan is the third part of a three-story series about Pia, Dragos, and their son, Liam. Each story stands alone, but fans might want to read all three: *Dragos Goes to Washington, Pia Does Hollywood,* and *Liam Takes Manhattan.*

Liam Takes Manhattan

(A Story of the Elder Races)

Thea Harrison

Liam Takes Manhattan
Copyright © 2015 by Teddy Harrison LLC
ISBN 10: 0-9906661-9-0
ISBN 13: 978-0-9906661-9-6
Print Edition

Cover Art © Frauke Spanuth

Chapter One

LIAM STOOD AT the edge of the rooftop of Cuelebre Tower, looking down at the city streets.

It was the darkest time of the year, after winter solstice and the annual Masque of the Gods, and right before Christmas. Below, the streets were decorated with Christmas lights, the ribbons of brilliant color piercing the frigid darkness.

Dense, icy snowflakes swirled on a wind so cold, it stabbed at the skin like tiny, invisible needles and whipped through his shaggy hair. He ran his fingers through it, but it tangled again immediately after. He needed a haircut, but when had there been time?

It was not just the darkest time of the year. It was also one of the darkest times for the Wyr. For the first time in history, a sentinel had fallen. Constantine was dead, killed in a battle with a first-generation Djinn.

Just a few days ago, they had burned his body on a funeral pyre. Shocked by a loss too deep for tears, the Wyr in the Tower went about their business like automatons, going through the motions. Dragos had decreed that the Masque would still be held, and so they'd done their jobs. Amidst the lavish festival, condolences poured in from all the other demesnes, while the Wyr endured.

Behind Liam, the rooftop door opened twenty feet away, and a soft footstep sounded. Recognizing the footstep, along with the hint of scent carried to him by the knifelike wind, Liam didn't turn around.

His mother stepped beside him, wrapped against the winter night in an ankle-length woolen coat, gloves and a cashmere scarf. As a gust of wind hit her, she shivered and lifted her collar to protect her neck as she looked out over the city.

"I don't know how you or your father can stand being out in this kind of weather without a coat," Pia muttered. "Just looking at you standing there in your T-shirt and jeans makes me feel cold."

Both he and his father carried so much fire inside, no winter chill could affect them.

"It feels good," he said, lifting his face to the wind. The light sting of snow on his skin broke through the distance between himself and the world.

Out of the corner of his eye, he saw his mother nod. Pia Cuelebre was a beautiful woman, tall and slender, with pale skin, light gold hair and dark violet eyes. She shone gently like a candle in the night.

After a few moments, she said, "Supper's ready."

"I'm not hungry." He turned his gaze back to the illuminated streets below. The dragon that lived inside him watched the small, fragile creatures with sharp interest.

"Liam," she said gently. "Please come downstairs and eat something. I don't think I've seen you take a bite since Con's funeral."

While that might be true, it wasn't exactly accurate. His mom had been overwhelmed with funeral preparations and her duties as hostess for the Masque, so the family hadn't shared very many meals like they normally did. Whenever she had checked on him, he hadn't been hungry.

But that didn't mean he hadn't eaten. Driven by instinct and need over the last week, he had shapeshifted into his dragon form and flown over the ocean repeatedly, hunting for massive amounts of food and gorging until he couldn't swallow another bite.

Now, her concern pressed against him like a cage, and he had to fight a small, fierce battle with himself to keep from lashing out at her. The events of the last week had brought his feral side too close to the surface, and he realized that he had become more dangerous.

Battle, his dragon whispered to him, as it had ever since he had learned of Con's death. *Fight. Death.*

Family, he told it. *Home. Love.*

The battle was over, and they had won. But at such a price.

His mom loved him and only wanted the best for him. And he loved her too. He would not give his feral side free rein and hurt her unnecessarily.

He told her, "I've eaten."

The tense line of her shoulders eased. "Well, that

makes me feel a little better, but you haven't eaten with us, so I'd like to see some of that action with my own eyes. You're ... you're growing so rapidly right now, you must need a lot of fuel."

For the first time since she had joined him, he turned fully to look down at her. Pia stood five-foot-ten, and he had passed that height yesterday.

Because in the darkest part of this particularly dark year, he had lost part of the battle with his dragon.

He had always been prone to growth spurts during times of crisis, and sometimes he'd had to fight to keep his dragon form under control as it strained to become fully grown.

All predator Wyr grew faster and stronger than other Wyr, and the dragon was the apex of the predators. Fueled by the unique magics he had inherited from both his parents, he had grown in massive bursts since his birth, lunging into life.

As he faced her, Pia drew in a breath. Tilting her head up to him, she whispered, "You're nearly as tall as your father."

One corner of his mouth lifted in a wry tilt. "I know."

"Do you ... can you tell if you're going to grow any taller?"

He hesitated and flexed his shoulders, considering. "I'm not sure, but I think I'm almost done."

Her violet gaze had turned wide with fascination. "I can only imagine what your dragon form must look like now."

"It's pretty big," he admitted.

"You'll have to show him to me soon." She tucked her hand into the crook of his arm and turned with him toward the stairwell. "In the meantime, let's get inside where it's warm. Your father and I want to talk to you."

Reluctantly he gave up the wild solitude of the night and went with her downstairs to the penthouse.

Huge though the penthouse was, the walls and warmth felt as confining as his parents' concern, but he endured being inside for her sake. The living room lay mostly in shadows, except for the brilliant multicolored lights glowing on the Christmas tree in the corner.

Pia had been half human before she had accessed her Wyr nature and successfully changed into her Wyr form. As a child, she had celebrated both the Masque and Christmas with her mother, and she had continued that tradition when she became Dragos's mate.

As a result, Christmas decorations filled both the penthouse and their home in upstate New York. Dragos had been content to indulge her, and had joined in the preparations. Stacks of colorfully wrapped presents lay underneath the tree.

Once inside, Pia pulled away and hurried down the hall toward the brightly lit kitchen and dining room. Liam paused momentarily, his dragon's eyes appreciating the lavish decorations and bright jewel-like colors adorning the tree before he strolled to catch up with her.

He knew his father was in the dining room before he

rounded the corner. Whenever they were in close proximity, Liam always knew where Dragos was. He could sense Dragos's Power in his mind's eye, like a burning sun. He wondered if his father could sense him in the same way.

Dragos stood at the head of the dining table, his attention focused on the large beef roast on the platter in front of him as he carved it into thin slices. Light from the overhead chandelier gleamed off his black hair and outlined his tall, broad-shouldered figure against the plate glass window behind him.

Porcelain clinked in the kitchen as Pia prepared other dishes. A brief surge of revulsion hit Liam at the sight and smell of the roast. He had eaten so much raw prey lately, the cooked meat looked vaguely revolting.

His dragon focused on the sharp knife his father wielded with such competent, lethal dexterity. Carefully, Liam throttled the beast back. He and his father loved each other too.

Dragos never lifted his head from his task. He said in a quiet voice, "Tell me you're in control, and I will believe you."

He hesitated. Of course his father would sense how close to the surface his dragon was. Dragos had been Lord of the Wyr for a very long time. No doubt he had dealt with many Wyr struggling with the feral side of their natures.

Straightening his shoulders, Liam replied steadily, "I'm in control."

Dragos's piercing gold gaze stabbed at him. Then his father turned his attention back to carving the roast. "Good enough. Go help your mom."

At the order, rebellion surged through him like a flash fire.

He thought, I'm not a child anymore. I won't do everything you tell me to do just because you tell me to do it.

As quickly as it hit, the rebellion subsided again, leaving him rueful and wary. Perhaps he wasn't quite as in control as he thought he was, or wanted to be.

Silently, he obeyed, walking into the kitchen to wash his hands. Afterward, he picked up serving platters filled with roasted sweet and white potatoes, Brussels sprouts sautéed in garlic and olive oil, and gravy.

Pia was just putting the finishing touches on her own meal, a vegan roast with vegan gravy. As he carried the food to the dining room, she gave him a grateful look.

With the quick ease of familiarity, they were soon seated. Dragos and Pia had wine. They didn't offer him any, and why would they? He was less than a year old. To them, he was a gigantic, dangerous child.

But he wasn't a child. Not any longer. He was young, very young and inexperienced, but no longer a child. Bitterness whipped through him at the thought. He throttled that back too. He was fast growing tired of this constant battle with himself.

After passing the food around, he took note when his mom and dad exchanged a look.

Here it is, he thought as he toyed with his food with a fork. Whatever it is they want to say to me.

Dragos turned to him. "Your mom and I want to apologize."

Taken aback, he blinked. "Apologize for what?"

Pia said, "We swore we wouldn't let this happen, but we got too busy and time slipped away from us. We had come to a decision a few months ago, but with the new pregnancy, and the trips to Washington DC and Los Angeles, and then getting ready for the Masque, and—and Con's death—" Her voice wobbled then firmed again. "Well, the last few months have been really hectic."

"I know," he replied, eyeing both of them cautiously. He had no idea where this conversation was going. "You've been more busy than usual. I get it. What's wrong?"

At that, Dragos and Pia exchanged another, longer look, their expressions too complex for him to read. Pia turned to him and said in a quiet voice, "Nothing new is wrong, my love. A few months ago we decided to let you have a dog, but we haven't had time to do anything about it. We want to get you a puppy for Christmas. Would you enjoy that?"

Carefully he set down his fork and repeated, "You want to get me a puppy."

"You've wanted a dog so badly," Pia said. While her face and voice remained mild, he noticed she hadn't touched her food either. "But your dad thinks it's best if you start with a puppy, so that it can get acclimated to the predator Wyr it would be living with. I compiled a list of breeders that we could visit next week, if you like."

Liam put his flattened hands on the table, on either side of his plate, and considered them. They were broad across the palm and long-fingered, like his father's. Then he pushed to his feet, strode into the kitchen and retrieved a wineglass. When he walked back into the dining room, his parents hadn't moved, but the atmosphere in the room had grown tense.

They watched in silence as he took the bottle of wine and poured himself a glass. Dragos's gaze flared into incandescence.

The wine was dark red, densely rich like rubies. Experimentally, he sipped it. It was dry, with the merest hint of blackberry and cherries. Gods, it was delicious. He took a deep swallow and returned to his seat.

"When you said you wanted to talk to me, do you know what I was expecting?" he said in a conversational tone. He looked at Dragos. "I was expecting either or both of you to try to talk me out of the pact you and I made when Con was killed."

His father lounged back in his seat, appearing to relax, but Liam knew he could move faster than almost any other Wyr, except for maybe his mom.

And him.

Dragos said, "I told you I would give you a year to prepare for a trial. Even if it goes against my better judgment, I won't back out of that."

"All I can think about is that a few days of that year are already gone," Liam said. "And you want to give me a puppy."

While his mom continued to look composed, her shoulders slumped, and he knew he had struck some kind of blow. It made his stomach hurt, but he couldn't take the words back. There was an eight-hundred-pound elephant in the room, and his name was Liam. They had to confront it.

He picked up his glass of wine and drank again, noting how both Pia and Dragos tracked his movements and the wariness in their expressions.

"How did you feel when I got myself a glass of wine?" he asked. After waiting a beat for them to respond, he continued. "It felt wrong to you, didn't it? You wanted to stop me."

Pia pushed her plate away and leaned her elbows on the table. "I can't deny it looked odd," she replied. As she met his eyes, her own gaze was steady and unwavering. "It's also odd for me to look up into your face when we're standing side by side. This last growth spurt you've had is the most significant one yet, and we're going to have to go through another period of adjustment. Be patient with us—we'll get there."

But that was just it—time was trickling away, and he didn't think he could afford to be very patient.

His father had given him a year to prepare for the trial to become a sentinel. His dragon had flared to meet the challenge, but he needed both education and raw experience. And everywhere around him were shackles made of love and expectation.

He felt like he was living in a trap. The urge to fly away as fast and as hard as he could swept over him again.

"Thank you for supper," he said, as he pushed his chair back and stood. "But I'm afraid I'm not very hungry again."

"Sit down," Dragos said. "We're not done talking."

He gave his father a long, level look. Whatever Dragos saw in his expression made him stand too, until they stared at each other eye to eye. Dragos's hard cut features were shuttered, but his eyes blazed with light. Liam wondered if his own gaze blazed with the same fierce light.

Neither one backed down. The air between them boiled with heat.

Liam said in a soft, courteous voice, "I'm done talking for now. I'll let you know when I'm ready to talk again."

With that, he pivoted on one heel and walked out. He took the distance to the living room in long strides, but behind him, he could still hear Pia whisper, "Dragos, let him go."

That was all he had time to hear before he pushed out the door, ran up the stairs to the roof, exploded into his Wyr form and took to the sky.

✧　✧　✧

AS SOON AS she heard the penthouse door settle behind Liam, Pia slumped and put her face in her hands.

"I wondered what life would be like when he reached a rebellious stage," she muttered. "So now I know."

She just hadn't expected him to exercise such control. She had thought he would go through a teenage phase of shouting and slamming doors, and if anything that she and Dragos would laugh about it when they were alone.

This was something entirely different. Almost overnight, it seemed, he'd shot up in height and his shoulders expanded, while his youthful rounded features grew lean and chiseled. Always a handsome boy, he was now indisputably a handsome young man.

They only wanted the best for him. They tried to do whatever they could that would make him feel loved and happy, but tonight the appearance of maturity, along with his quiet voice, and the clenched effort in his demeanor had turned the whole encounter dark with a sense of desperation.

"This is a mistake," Dragos growled. "I'm going to withdraw my decision."

The tension in the room hadn't dissipated with Liam's departure. Dragos's energy was boiling furiously. It felt to Pia like a raw blast of heat.

She lifted her head to look at him. Now that they were alone, he looked tired, exasperated and more than a little angry.

The events of the last week had been brutal on everyone. Bereavement was hard at any time, but Con's death had been hardest on Dragos and the sentinels, who had lost a brother and a comrade-in-arms. Her heart ached for the tired slump in Dragos's shoulders and the shadows under his eyes.

But as long as he was Lord of the Wyr, it was his job to handle it. And because he had such broad, strong shoulders, she knew that he could.

So she didn't say anything to make it easier on him. Instead, she said, "Hold on. You made him a promise, and you have to keep it. No matter how hard it might be, we don't break promises we make to our children. You just told him so, yourself."

He shook his head. "Normally I would agree with you, but Liam can't be a rebellious son and expect to be a sentinel at the same time. I won't allow it. Sentinels obey orders. They have to, Pia."

Of course he was right. Sentinels were responsible for carrying out Dragos's orders, and they were responsible for the safety of the Wyr demesne. It was essential for them to be able to balance following orders with taking independent initiative when necessary.

But Dragos was only right up to a point.

"Well, he isn't a sentinel," she said dryly. She wasn't quite sure how to finish that sentence—Yet? Ever?—so she left it hanging awkwardly in the silence. "I guess that means he gets to be a rebellious son right now."

He looked at her, gold eyes blazing. "Point taken. Should I go after him?"

Dropping her head back into her hands, she scrubbed at her scalp with her fingers as she tried to think.

One of the things that made her so happy was the love she witnessed between father and son. But no matter how much love lay between them, Dragos was very much the autocrat, and Liam had already demonstrated he wasn't responding very well to that at the moment.

Finally she replied, "I think we need to let him be. And trust him. He's our good, sweet boy, and I know he will become a good, sweet man. Let's not make that transition harder on him than it has to be." Pressing her fingertips to her temples, she added, "I think."

Dragos dropped a hand onto her shoulder and squeezed lightly. His touch steadied her as it always did, and she reached behind her to cover his fingers with her own.

Then he sat down at the dining table, rubbed his face and said, "So I guess we eat dinner."

She nodded. "I guess we do."

She thought she had lost her appetite, but they had a new son growing inside her, and the demands he made on her body had her rethinking that almost immediately. As Dragos picked up his knife and fork, she drew her plate back to her, and they ate their meal in thoughtful, worried silence.

Chapter Two

M OST PEOPLE HAD no idea who Liam was.

Most of the public, if they had heard of Liam Cuelebre, prince of the Wyr, would think of him as the new addition to the Cuelebre family. They might remember the baby photos that his mom and dad had released to the media not a year ago. If anything, they would expect him to be approaching toddlerhood.

Even most of the Wyr who lived in Cuelebre Tower didn't know the tall, broad-shouldered Liam who had emerged over the last two days. After flying all night and turning over the puzzle pieces of his trap, he found an odd sort of comfort standing unrecognized in line at the Starbucks on the ground floor of the Tower.

The dark-haired girl standing in line in front of him was cute. Really cute. She wore a tunic and leggings, and her gazelle long legs were sheathed in narrow black boots.

Evidently, she thought he was pretty cute too, as she looked over her shoulder and gave him a shy smile. Male interest sparked in his tired mind. As he took a step closer and opened his mouth, someone tapped his shoulder.

When he turned, he found Hugh standing behind him. Instantly, the small pleasure of sharing a smile with a pretty girl evaporated, and the invisible trap sprang around him again.

"What's up, sport?" Hugh asked, his plain, bony face creased in a smile.

Hugh had been his babysitter and bodyguard for several months now. Retired from active duty in the Wyr military service, Hugh had a long rangy body, lethal combat skills and a mild, soft-spoken manner, and while Liam loved the gargoyle, the last thing he ever wanted to ask a girl he'd been about to invite out on a date was if she had met his nanny yet.

He snapped, "What are you doing here? Did Mom or Dad send you?"

Hugh's smile faded and his hand fell away. "No, I havna talked to them this morning." His Scottish accent was usually faint, but it sounded more pronounced when he was upset. "I was just getting in line to grab a cup of coffee and saw you standing here."

Remorse prickled Liam's conscience. Giving up on the idea of flirting with the girl in front of him, he rubbed the back of his neck and muttered, "Sorry. I didn't get any sleep, and I'm short-tempered right now."

"Don't worry about it," Hugh said. "It's been a tough week for everybody."

"Yeah, no kidding." Whenever Liam thought of Constantine's still face on the funeral pyre, he wanted to cry or fly into a rage. He had cried, in the dark of the night when he had been alone.

Con had been family too. He did not want to see the other male's death as an opportunity. He did not.

The line moved, and the girl walked away with her drink. Liam placed his order for a cup of black coffee and Hugh did too.

As they collected their drinks, Hugh walked over to the nearby stand to stir three packets of sugar into his coffee. Liam followed and hovered near Hugh's elbow, his thoughts and emotions as unsettled as they had been when he had left the penthouse the night before.

Without looking at him, Hugh asked quietly, "Feel like talking? Or do you have some place you've got to be?"

He knew his mom would be fretting about him, and probably his dad too, if Dragos fretted about anything. He needed to check in upstairs, but he wasn't ready to face them yet. Not until he managed to put himself in some kind of order and had at least some idea of what he needed to say, if not what the end result of the conversation might be.

Blowing out a breath, he replied, "Sure. I mean, if you've got the time. You're supposed to be off this week."

Hugh's rare smile appeared again, lighting up his face. "I always have time for you, sport. Come on."

Walking out of the Starbucks, Hugh led the way to the large open food court area by an indoor fountain.

Several tables were available. As they settled into chairs, Liam gulped at his coffee and looked around. He recognized several of the people at other tables, but nobody glanced at them or appeared to recognize him. By virtue of the acoustics and the noise of the fountain, the area was as good a place as any to have a private conversation.

Hugh removed the lid from his coffee and blew on it. "What's going on?"

"My life is all knotted up," Liam muttered. "And I don't know how to untangle it."

The gargoyle gave a slow, calm nod. "Why don't you start with one piece and let's see what happens."

The cute girl walked by. Slouching in his seat, Liam watched her until she was out of sight. He said, "I feel so damn guilty."

"What on earth do you have to feel guilty about?"

The surprised kindness in Hugh's expression brought unexpected tears springing to his eyes. Shoving his fingers through his overlong hair, he blinked rapidly until they disappeared.

Sometimes things felt so raw that they were almost impossible to say out loud, no matter how much privacy one had. He forced the words out through gritted teeth. "I feel sick that Constantine is dead, but I feel even sicker about the fact that he was barely cremated before I took advantage of it."

Hugh's gray eyes sharpened, and his expression turned very serious. "Liam," he said with quiet firmness.

"There is no way on earth anybody believes that you took advantage of Con's death."

Hunching his shoulders, Liam wrapped his hands around his hot coffee cup and stared down at it. His hands seemed like they belonged to a stranger now, large and powerful. He clenched them into fists.

"As soon as he was cremated, I started pushing my dad to let me fight for the empty sentinel position," he muttered. "And I didn't stop until he said yes. It was all I could think about. It's almost all I can think about right now too."

Hugh took a small, thoughtful sip from his coffee before he replied. "The way I heard it told, the sentinels asked Dragos what he was going to do to fill the position. You joined in the conversation. Nothing wrong with that, Liam. And there was nothing wrong with getting your dad to take you seriously enough to promise to at least give you a chance."

Every careful word Hugh said stung. But then everything stung these days. Liam rubbed his tired eyes and replied flatly, "You don't think I can do it, do you?"

He shouldn't be surprised. Nobody thought he could. Hell, even he wasn't sure if he could.

Dragos's seven sentinels were among the most deadly Wyr fighters in the world. They combined strength, cunning, ruthlessness and experience, and when they went after something, they did it with complete, unswerving dedication.

Liam had one huge asset in his favor—his dragon

form. Because of it, he was faster and more powerful than any of the other sentinels, but that didn't give him the experience he needed to win the empty position in a trial by combat. It didn't give him investigative skills, honed by years of work, or tactical battle experience.

He had virtually nothing he could take to the position except for raw magical skills and brute strength. And if there was one thing he would bet on, it was that his father would not pull any punches when it came down to a trial by combat to fill the vacancy.

If anything, Dragos would probably be more ruthless than ever, because he had made it crystal clear: he would not give Liam the position. He would give Liam almost anything else Liam asked for, but not that. Liam would have to earn it, like every other sentinel had earned their place, or he would be out.

And if he was out, he truly had no idea what he would do with his life. He was too Powerful, too unique. There was no place for him in the Wyr demesne that felt genuine.

Dragos had offered him a starter position in one of his companies, but that felt fake and unsatisfying. He didn't want to work for his father. As much as he loved him, he was very much aware that Dragos's age, reputation and Power meant he cast a very long shadow, and Liam didn't want to live under that. He wanted to fight, to claw his way to his own place in the world, and own it.

Searching his gaze, Hugh asked, "Do you even want the position? Because you should think long and hard about that. The sentinels live a hard life. Their lives are dangerous, and they're always on call, always. Getting hurt would be a way of life. Loneliness might well be a way of life too. There's a reason why none of them have mated until recently. It's a rare person who can genuinely, wholeheartedly commit to having a Wyr sentinel as their mate."

Liam's gaze went to the fountain. He said, "I think so. I mean, I think I want it. Fighting for the position, and winning it, and facing those daily challenges sounds … satisfying. But how can I know for sure? The possibility didn't even come up until this week. All I really know for sure is that I want the chance to try for it, even if it seems unlikely that I'll get it." The bitterness crept back into his voice. "Besides, what else am I going to do?"

"First," Hugh said, "feeling at a loss as to what to do with your life is something every young person goes through, Liam, so take heart. As unique as some of your challenges might be, you're also going through something verra normal. Second—you can't become a sentinel just because you don't know what else to do with your life."

He closed his eyes. "I know."

"You've got a lot to think about."

"Yeah. And somehow I've got to find the right kind of training. The training that you and the sentinels have given me has been great, but—it's not enough. You guys love me. I need the kind of experience where somebody's not going to give a shit if they knock my teeth in. I need to go through real life, live with real danger."

Hugh pursed his lips. "That's not going to be the easiest thing to come by. You also need space to think, and while you might not want to admit this, Liam, you still need some schooling. You're so talented and book bright, and you have a lot of facts crammed into that extremely capacious head of yours, but you don't have real-life application."

"I know," he muttered again. His shoulders slumped. The challenges he faced felt all but insurmountable. "I have no idea how to get any of that. I just . . ." He took a deep breath and forced himself to say what had haunted him all through the sleepless night. "I don't think I can get any of that at home."

The older man studied him in long silence. Then he leaned forward, bracing his elbows on the table, and said softly, "I'm going to tell you something that, well, nobody told me *not* to tell you. But at the same time, I dinna think your mom and dad would take too kindly that I *do* tell you, so I would appreciate it if you and I can keep this between ourselves. Can you do that?"

Liam's attention sharpened. He replied, "Sure. Whatever you say stays between the two of us."

"Okay." Hugh rubbed his face with one large raw-boned hand. "Have you ever heard of Glenhaven?"

Liam frowned, searching his memory, and came up with a vague reference he had heard at some point. "Isn't that a Scottish college?"

"Yes, it is. More accurately, Glenhaven is *the* college for the Elder Races. It's not actually in Scotland, but in an Other land, with the crossover passageway located just outside of Edinburgh. While the college is run by the gargoyle clans, it's not affiliated with any one demesne or race. When you were very small, yet still clearly showing what a prodigy you were, Dragos and Pia had a brief discussion about whether or not they should send you to Glenhaven."

He frowned, the vague memory teasing him. Was that where he had heard the name? Had he overheard his mom and dad discussing it? "They never said anything about it to me."

"That's because they quickly ruled it out as an option. At the start of each term, Glenhaven closes the crossover passageway. Nobody gets in or out until the term is over. The school claims that blocking access to the outside allows them to maintain their impartiality and high academic standards. It's also supposed to create an atmosphere where students develop their own relationships with each other, with a minimum of influence from outside politics. I think the real truth is that people take their political biases with them into the college, but that's neither here nor there, I guess."

As Liam listened, his mind began to race. "If the college is in an Other land, time doesn't pass there like it does for us. What's the time slippage like?"

Hugh shrugged. "I've heard time passes faster for the college than it does on Earth, but I don't know any actual numbers."

"If time passes faster there, I could possibly get more time to prepare," Liam said, beginning to feel the first stirrings of excitement. "It would be pushing at the terms of Dad's promise, but it's worth considering."

"I think it is," Hugh replied, giving him a sidelong smile. "There are disadvantages too, though. It's a long way away. If you went to Glenhaven, you would be completely cut off from everything and everyone you've known in your life. There's no phone calls home. No email, no Internet, no microwave popcorn, cars or movies. No changing your mind, at least until the end of a term. For those reasons alone, I don't think Pia and Dragos did more than discuss it once or twice and ask me a few questions about it. Also, you might squander a significant portion of your year on something that you find doesn't meet all your needs the way you had hoped, or help you get ready to face the sentinel trial."

Absorbing the information, he nodded. Going to Glenhaven would be a risk. But it might be his best shot to figure out what the hell he needed to do with his life.

Liam asked, "Have you been to Glenhaven before?"

The older man shook his head. "No, I haven't. I'm not from any of the clans that run the college. I have seen drawings and paintings, though, and they look quite beautiful. They have some images posted on their website, if you want to take a look."

"I do," he said absently, as his mind raced through possibilities. Then he caught up with what Hugh had said, and laughed. "They're based in an Other land, yet they have a website?"

The gargoyle chuckled. "Yeah, it's not an extensive website like academic institutions here have, with web portals, online databases and class curriculums. But it does offer some general descriptions. Tuition fees are pretty astronomical, or so I've heard, but I think they also have scholarship programs for intellectually and magically gifted individuals. It's not just the wealthy and privileged of the Elder Races that attend."

"I need to get to a laptop." Tossing back the last of his coffee, Liam stood, and Hugh did as well. He paused to give the other man an earnest look. "Thank you. Seriously. I really needed this conversation."

Hugh's smile creased his lean cheeks. Hooking an arm around Liam's neck, Hugh pulled him into a brief, tight hug. "You're most welcome, sport. I'm glad it helped. I'm going to get some breakfast. Want to join me?"

He shook his head as he returned Hugh's hug with enthusiasm. "Can't. I've got too much to do."

Along with a conversation he needed to have with his parents.

"Call if you need anything else."

"I will," Liam promised. "Talk to you later?"

"Any time."

As they parted, Hugh strolled back to the Starbucks line. Liam strode toward the nearby bank of elevators. Then he paused. While his dad probably had too much to do in the aftermath of Constantine's passing, he would bet money that his mother was spending time in the penthouse, keeping watch for his return.

He still wasn't ready to talk. Not quite yet.

Digging out his phone, he typed out a text. Hi Mom. I love you.

Almost immediately, his phone pinged in reply. I love you too. How are you doing?

Pretty good. His thumbs moved rapidly across the small screen. I've been getting my head sorted out. I have a few things I need to do, but can we talk at noon?

Of course. Do you need anything?

He smiled. No. But thank you.

You're welcome. You know I'd do anything for you, right? Just say the word.

Yeah. I do know. Talk to you soon.

Once he hit send on the final message, he tucked his phone back into the pocket of his jeans, swiveled and headed out the wide glass doors. The public library would be opening soon. He could use one of their computers to find out more about Glenhaven.

And, just for the hell of it, he might do a little Internet searching on dogs while he was at it.

Chapter Three

SEVERAL HOURS LATER, right at noon, Liam walked into the penthouse to find his mother and father waiting in the living room.

Dragos sat in an armchair nearest the Christmas tree, reading a book on ancient Egyptian treasure, one ankle hooked over his knee and a cup of aromatic coffee on the nearby table. Pia curled up at one end of the couch, flipping through a magazine. The scene looked peaceful and inviting, and they looked quite calm.

Calm was good. Calm was super good.

Dragos was also present in the middle of a workday, during a highly stressed time, so Liam knew just what a priority his parents had placed on talking to him.

As Liam entered, Dragos laid his book on the table, and Pia straightened to set her magazine aside.

Tucking his hands in his pockets, Liam strolled over to throw himself down on the couch beside Pia.

He said, "Hi."

"Hi, sweetheart." She gave him a wry smile. "You know I have to ask it—are you hungry?"

"No, thanks. I picked up a sandwich when I was

out." He returned her smile with a crooked one of his own before he said to Dragos, "I'm sorry to interrupt your workday."

"It's no trouble." Dragos reached for his coffee cup. "You are always going to be one of my highest priorities."

Yeah, he knew that. Once he could get his dragon side to calm down, he could even feel it. Liam was uneasy with how his dragon bristled when his father got too commanding. Dragos was not just a powerful personality. He was a ruler. Rulers tended to get commanding and dictatorial from time to time.

He said, "I have some things to say."

Pia laid a hand on his knee. "You can tell us anything. You know that."

"Yeah, I do." He squeezed her hand and took a deep breath. "First, I wanted to say thank you, and it's my turn to apologize. Things haven't been easy on anybody, but even through that, you guys have been super patient with me, and you've given me space when I needed it. I really appreciate it, and I'm sorry if I've added to your stress this week."

Dragos waved that aside. "Don't concern yourself with that."

Even though Dragos meant nothing but good, and Liam's dragon had calmed considerably, it still bristled at his father's autocratic way of wording things. He choked his reaction down.

Now that he was nearing maturity, would it always

feel that way between them? They were two male dragons, both territorial, both possessive.

As much as he'd had to wrestle with himself lately, it would have been handy if he could have split himself in two, because sometimes he simply wanted to put his hands around the neck of his dragon and throttle it.

Pia asked, "The important question is, are you feeling better?"

He nodded. "I flew around all night and did a lot of thinking. Then I talked to a few people and researched some stuff."

"Who did you talk to?" Dragos asked.

Now it was his turn to wave that away. "That's not important. The main thing is, it helped."

"Good." Dragos said, "What else?"

Here we go.

"Thank you for offering to get me a puppy." He looked at both of them in turn. "It was really thoughtful of you. I did some thinking about that too, and I'd like to turn your gift into something bigger, if that's okay."

Pia's gaze went wide with interest. "What did you have in mind?"

"I want lots and lots of dogs. Sort of." He gave them a crooked grin. "I'd like for you to buy West River Animal Shelter."

Dragos's eyes narrowed. "You want us to buy an animal shelter? Your mom already donates to several already."

Liam turned to Pia. "Yes, I know, but you only donate to no-kill shelters, right?"

"Of course," she said.

"West River doesn't have a no-kill policy," he told her. "I want us to buy it and turn it into a no-kill shelter so that one way or another, every dog that goes there gets a home."

Pia started to smile, and her eyes shone. She whirled to Dragos, who inclined his head and made an acquiescing gesture.

Dragos said, "As long as you two take care of all the details, I have no objections."

Liam grinned. "Thanks for the Christmas present."

"You are the most outstanding son anybody could ever wish for," Pia said as she threw her arms around him. "I love that idea so much, and I have no idea how to go about doing it."

"Are you kidding?" Dragos said dryly. "They will be ecstatic to get this offer. You do realize it will probably mean ongoing donations just to keep the shelter afloat."

"That's okay, I'll add it to my list," Pia said. She said to Liam, "You'll help me with things, won't you?"

"I'll help you as much as I can," Liam told her. "But that kinda leads me to the last thing I need to tell you." Dragos raised his eyebrows, and Pia looked at him expectantly. He braced himself. "This morning I applied to Glenhaven College."

Pia's face went blank with surprise. She said, "You did what?"

Dragos's expression darkened. He sat forward. "You

applied to Glenhaven without talking to us?"

It was harder than he had expected to meet his father's blazing gaze, but he couldn't back down now. He said steadily, "Yes, I did."

"Absolutely not," Dragos snapped. "You're not going to Glenhaven. I forbid it."

Whoops, there was no throttling back his dragon at that one.

Liam snapped in reply, "You can't forbid me to go!"

Anger burned in his father's eyes. He snarled, "I can sure as hell refuse to pay for it!"

What the hell? "I didn't ask you to pay for anything!"

"Stop it," Pia said.

"You just asked me to pay for an animal shelter," Dragos shot back.

"What, are you going to refuse to do that now?" Liam felt his fists clenching. "So I guess I only get Christmas presents or college when I do what you say?"

Pia leaped to her feet and shouted, "*Stop it, both of you!*"

There was so much passion and forcefulness in her voice, both Liam and Dragos stopped to stare at her. Her face was clenched, and tears stood in her eyes.

She pointed at Dragos. "You are saying things in the heat of anger, and you're going to regret them." Then she turned to Liam and told him fiercely, "Of course you get Christmas presents and college. But both of you need to take care right now. Remember that you love each other and act that way."

Unable to sit still any longer, Liam threw himself to his feet and started to pace. "I don't understand why you're trying to forbid me to go. It's the only option open to me that makes any sense."

"You'll have to pick another college," Dragos snapped. "Somewhere more accessible—maybe Harvard, or Yale. Glenhaven is far too remote and too secluded. If something were to happen, you wouldn't be able to get in touch with us. We wouldn't be able to get in contact with you, or help you."

Right now that sounded like heaven to him.

Liam forced himself to breathe evenly and managed not to say it. Instead, he said, "Harvard and Yale aren't appropriate, so if something were to happen, you'll just have to trust me to handle it."

Dragos shook his head. "You're too young."

"If you can't trust me to go away to college by myself," he said through gritted teeth, "then you sure as hell can't trust me to become a sentinel. But you're not expecting me to become a sentinel anyway—are you?"

His father said nothing. But then he didn't have to. His silence said it all.

Tired tears sprang to Liam's eyes, and he spun away to hide it.

"Look," Pia said, her voice sounding a little ragged. "College is a good idea for anybody, and so is finding independence. But Liam, there are a lot of reasons why your dad and I are not reacting well to this, especially after our trip to the Light Fae demesne last month."

He turned slightly at that. "What do you mean?"

"Before Tatiana split from the Seelie Court to form her demesne in Los Angeles, her twin sister Isabeau, the Light Fae Queen of the Seelie Court, and Dragos shared some kind of past together, and your father can't remember anything about it."

That brought him all the way around again. Frowning, he met Dragos's gaze. "Is that part of your memory loss from the construction accident a few months ago?"

"Yes," Dragos said, his voice edged. "Apparently I spent some time at the Seelie Court, and I don't know if Isabeau and I parted as friends or not. All we really know is that Isabeau is very dangerous, and so is her private army. After watching her attack on her sister's demesne, it's clear that she's not inclined to be a forgiving sort of woman. The United Kingdom isn't the safest place for a Cuelebre to be, Liam."

Exasperated, Liam flung up both hands. "The United Kingdom is a big place, Dad. Not only that, but Glenhaven closes their passageway during every term."

Dragos folded his arms. "The United Kingdom might be a big place, but in many ways, the Elder Races world is a small one. Being my son will attract a lot of attention wherever you go."

Quickly, Liam crossed the living room. He said eagerly, "But that's the beauty of this—I don't want to go to college as a Cuelebre."

Pia stared at him. "Why not?"

He couldn't keep his fists from clenching again, as he

said, "For the exact reason Dad just brought up. Please don't take this the wrong way, but you are a really hard act to follow. Your reputation is—well, it's just everywhere. There's no place I can go to escape it if I go as Liam Cuelebre."

Dragos's expression didn't change, but he blinked. He said roughly, "I didn't know you were having a problem with being my son, or that you felt the need to escape."

Agh. Now he had managed to hurt both his parents. Way to go, asshole.

Forcing his way past his own frustration, he reached for gentleness. "That's not what I meant. I love you, and I am proud to be your son. I'm just finding it difficult to live in your shadow. I have to figure out my own way to go in life." He looked at Pia. "I used your maiden name. I set up a new email address, rented a P.O. box, and I filled out the Glenhaven application as Liam Giovanni. I'm pretty sure that guy doesn't have a reputation anywhere that he needs to watch out for." He paused, and then in as neutral a tone as he could manage, he added, "Not only that, but he would probably qualify for either an academic or magical scholarship."

With that, he put everything out there. He knew he was gifted intellectually and magically. While he didn't come right out and say it, the information made it clear—he didn't need his parents' money to go to college. He didn't need their approval.

And he could see in their expressions that they knew

it too. Pia blinked rapidly as she absorbed everything he said, while Dragos rubbed his forehead.

Liam's chest felt funny, heavy and dull. He walked over to the couch to sit beside his mom again and put his arm around her. As she leaned against his side, he hugged her and whispered, "I've really thought this through, and I want you to be happy for me."

"Okay," Dragos said suddenly. Both Pia and Liam turned to him in surprise.

"Okay?" Liam asked, hardly daring to hope. "You mean, it's okay if I go?"

"I've listened to your argument, and I've changed my mind. I think you're right." Dragos leaned forward, his elbows on his knees, and his hard-edged face looked alert. He looked at Pia. "This idea will work. We've always protected Liam's privacy, and we've kept a tight lid on his growth spurts. Even those who do know wouldn't necessarily recognize him after this latest one. Look at him. He looks more like you than he does me."

Nodding, Pia wiped her face. She said to Liam, "You would have to keep your Wyr form a secret. Sometimes that takes some tap dancing so you would have to stay on your guard, but you can do it."

"And I won't hear another word about you taking a scholarship," Dragos added. "You're my son. I will pay for your college, and living expenses, and anything else you need while you're in school."

This time, his father's autocratic way of speaking didn't bother him in the slightest. The heavy dull feeling eased, to be replaced by a rush of emotion so intense, tears sprang to his eyes again.

He muttered around a lump in his throat, "Thanks."

"Of course"—Dragos met his gaze—"I have stipulations."

Stipulations were fine. They were good—they weren't an outright refusal. "Oh yeah?" he replied. "Like what?"

"I want an undercover presence in Glenhaven, and another one in Edinburgh to protect the entrance to the crossover passageway. And you don't linger or go on a UK walkabout between terms. There's no sense in taking unnecessary chances. You go in, and when you come out, you leave Scotland entirely."

That all sounded reasonable. He nodded. "I can do that."

Pia said, "If you're sure that this is what's best for you, we'll help you any way we can. And we'll be here waiting when you're ready to come home."

Relief had him leaning sideways so that his head and shoulders fell into her lap. He muttered telepathically in her head, *I hate arguing with you.*

Well, technically, you argued with your dad, she told him, while she ran her fingers through his hair. *But I get your point. And I hated it too. Are we all better now?*

Comfort stole through him at her gentle touch, and he nodded again.

I'm proud of you, she told him.

Twisting onto his back, he looked up into her face.

You are?

You thought things through, you used your best judgment and took independent action as the situation needed, and you didn't take no for an answer. She smiled down at him. *And who knows what the future will bring. After going to school, you might decide that you don't want to try for the sentinel position after all. But if you still want to—you know, all of those things that you just did are good qualities for a sentinel to have.*

They are?

Yes, they are.

For the first time in a week, he didn't feel the compulsion to fly away. Things had started to feel right again, and that allowed tiredness to take over. A huge yawn cracked his face.

Nearby, chair springs creaked as Dragos stood. He said, "I have to get back to work. Don't hold dinner for me. I think it's going to be a late night."

Pia nodded and said, "Okay. I'll have something waiting for you in the fridge."

Dragos stepped forward to bend over Liam and kiss his forehead. Liam looked up into his father's fierce gold gaze.

Dragos said, "You are unexpectedly stubborn and resourceful. You're also a good boy, and I'm sorry I lost my temper. And I'm sorry you had to push to get us to recognize what you needed and wanted from us."

"It's all good," Liam said. "I mean, it's not like you guys were experts on what to do with a magically growing kid."

"Well, we're the only experts there are," Dragos told him wryly.

Liam grinned up at him, so happy not to be arguing with his dad anymore. Just plain stinking happy. "And I'm going to college!"

"Yes," his father said, returning his smile. "It appears that you are."

Chapter Four

WHEN EXHAUSTION SET in, it was sudden and fierce. Liam went to bed early and slept in late. The only reason he woke up at all was because Pia knocked on his door and then walked into his room.

"Get up, sleepyhead!" she said.

"*Mmph*," he grunted, and pulled his pillow over his head.

She dragged the bedcovers off his body. "I mean it—get up!"

"Moooooom, it's too early," he complained. "You sound disgustingly cheerful, and I don't need those covers anyway."

"It's not early—it's almost ten o'clock, Liam. Here, I brought you a cup of coffee."

He could smell the coffee from underneath his pillow, dark, rich and alluring. "Get thee behind me, Satan," he said experimentally.

She burst out laughing. "Where on earth did you hear that?"

"Some woman muttered it yesterday when she was looking at the pastries at Starbucks." Light fingers tickled his bare feet, and he jackknifed to a sitting position. "*Hey!* You cheated!"

"There's your beautiful face," she said cheerfully. She had set the coffee mug on his bedside table. "If you get up and shower right now, you'll have enough time to eat breakfast before we go to the West River Animal Shelter to meet with the executive director, Eileen Riley."

"What?" He stared at her then grabbed up the coffee cup. "But it's Christmas Eve!"

She opened her eyes wide. "I know, right? I emailed them a basic inquiry yesterday afternoon, but I wasn't expecting to hear back from them until after the holidays. Eileen just called me, and she would love to talk. Apparently they're having some serious financial difficulties, and she's willing to consider almost anything to keep the doors open. She said my email was the Christmas miracle they'd been hoping for." Pia paused and tilted her head. "You didn't by any chance know anything about that somehow, did you?"

"No," he said. He gulped coffee and stood up. "I just did some quick searches on Yelp and a reference librarian helped me compile a list of shelters. Then I checked addresses, and West River was close enough that I could stop by from time to time to see how things are going."

"Well, hurry up," she told him. "We leave in forty-five minutes. And we have to get you a haircut sometime today. You're starting to look like a sulky rock star."

"Well, I *am* a rock star," he said, deadpan.

She laughed. "That you are."

Galvanized into action, he showered in record time and dressed in jeans, lumberjack-style boots and a navy blue, ribbed pullover sweater. When he strode into the kitchen Pia had another cup of coffee waiting for him, along with a huge sandwich. He leaned back against the counter, took a large bite and said around his mouthful, "Where's Dad?"

"Working." A shadow fell over Pia's face.

He paused with the sandwich halfway to his mouth. "Is it stuff about Con?"

"Probably," she said. The shadow passed, and she smiled at him. "He said if he can get away for an hour, he would join us in a bit. Not to look at the animals, of course. The poor things would be terrified of him."

"I won't go look at them either," he muttered, as he finished his breakfast in record time. "They'll be terrified of me too."

Pia dumped his dishes into the sink. "You never know, they might have some puppies and kittens that you can visit with. Let's go."

He grabbed his leather jacket, she slipped into her coat, and together, they went downstairs where Pia's guard and friend Eva waited with a warm car. Pia climbed into the front passenger seat while Liam took the backseat. He watched the snowy city streets scroll past while the two women chatted.

Hopefully soon, someone from Glenhaven would read his application and get in touch with him. The college had three terms a year, and the next term started directly after New Year's. His stomach knotted with equal parts fear and excitement.

I might be leaving home in a few weeks, he thought. That is, if Glenhaven has any room for new students. What if there's a waitlist? What if I can't get in for a year?

It was the first time he had considered the possibility, and the thought was unwelcome. He knew he was privileged and lucky in so many ways. For the most part, things happened the way he needed them to, and if for some reason they didn't, his parents moved heaven and earth to make sure they did.

But Liam Giovanni didn't have that kind of support. He couldn't, not and still keep his identity a secret.

He blurted out, "What if I don't get in?"

Pia and Eva fell silent for a moment. Eva asked, "Get in where?"

"I'll fill you in on everything later," Pia told her. Twisting in her seat to look at him, Pia said, "Honey, all any admissions counselor has to do is see how you can run fire up and down your hands and arms, while not getting burned. Believe me, they'll let you in. They'll probably try to shove a scholarship at you too, no matter what your father says."

His panic subsided a bit. He muttered, "I sure hope so."

"Try not to worry." Pia reached back to pat his knee. "Everything is going to be okay."

Her reassurance helped, but only a little. Because

what if it wasn't? Sometimes things weren't okay. People died, and bad things happened.

A shiver ran down his spine, but he slid into silence again, crossing his arms and hunching in his seat as much as his seat belt would let him as he stared out the window.

West River Animal Shelter was located in a rundown industrial area in the southeast section of Midtown West, just north of the Lincoln Tunnel and close to the Hudson River. There wasn't a parking lot, so as Eva looked for a place to park, Pia turned around to Liam again.

"If you're going to college as Liam Giovanni, we have to start working now to keep your identity a secret. We can't tell anybody at the shelter about you." Pia's gaze was serious as she searched his expression. "We can't explain that my magical son wanted us to buy the organization. As far as most of the world knows, you're still a baby."

"Yeah, I get it," he said. "I'm cool with that."

"And besides, I don't even know if you can buy a nonprofit. We'll probably have to make a large enough donation so that we can get a seat on the board and change policy from there."

"I'm cool with that too," he said. "I just want to change it so that it has a no-kill policy."

"Well, one way or another, we'll get that done." She smiled at him. "And in the meantime, you need to be one of my guards for this trip. Okay?"

He shrugged. "Sure."

Finally, Eva located a spot and backed into it, and Liam opened his door to step out on the snow-packed street. He followed Pia and Eva into the utilitarian-looking building, while he noted how Eva's restless dark gaze never seemed to stop roaming.

Eva had been an excellent soldier. She had commanded the unit that Hugh had been in, and now she made just as excellent a bodyguard. But she would never make a sentinel. What was the difference?

Eva was a canine Wyr, and her lifespan was nowhere near that of one of the immortals, but that wasn't the difference. Dragos didn't make a distinction between the immortal Wyr and the others—Eva was just as welcome as anybody else to try for a sentinel position if she wanted it, and if she won the position, it would be hers for as long as she could do her job.

No, it was something else. Perhaps it was fire.

Eva didn't have the drive to become a sentinel. While she had alpha tendencies, she had been content to be a unit commander, and she liked being Pia's bodyguard. But Liam couldn't imagine any of the sentinels being content with such a position for long, even though they liked to wear a laid-back demeanor.

So aside from ability, experience and ruthlessness, did a sentinel need to be driven as well? And if so, did Liam have that kind of fire in him for the position?

All he knew for certain was that he was going to be asking himself a lot of questions during the upcoming year.

Inside, the large lobby was utilitarian as well. Somebody had tried to make up for it by painting the concrete block walls with bright colors, and a large fake Christmas tree stood in one corner, decorated with pet toys and leashes.

They walked to the front reception desk where Pia gave her name. The elderly receptionist spoke on the phone and then told them that the executive director would be out in just a moment.

Smells assaulted Liam's sensitive nose—disinfectant, along with the scents of stressed animals. A man and two young girls walked past them with a border collie mix on leash. As it neared Liam, the dog shrieked and tried to pull out of its collar.

His heart sinking, he quickly retreated until the family could calm the dog enough to walk it out the front door. Out of the corner of his eye, he saw his mom give him a sad look before Pia turned to the front receptionist and asked, "Do you have a section with puppies?"

"We sure do," the receptionist told her. "All the puppies that are up for adoption are through that glass door. You'll be able to see it in a moment. I'm sure Eileen will want to give you a tour."

"Certainly," Pia said. She looked at Liam and told him telepathically, *Go visit with the puppies if you want.*

He hesitated. *You don't mind?*

Of course not. She smiled at him. *We'll just be talking about annual budgets and policy changes anyway. Go—enjoy yourself. I've got this.*

Thanks. As a brisk gray-haired woman strode up to Pia and Eva, Liam stuck his hands in the pockets of his jeans and strolled over to the glass door that led to the area where the adoptable puppies were kept.

On the other side of the door, a long room held a series of pens with waist-high gates. High squeaks and yaps sounded as he approached.

He peered over the first gate, but that kennel was empty. The next held three sleeping Chihuahua puppies, curled in a pile on a folded blanket. He smiled as he looked at their small, round bellies.

The third kennel held two Rottweiler mix puppies that rolled along the floor and play-fought with each other. He clicked his tongue at them and snapped his fingers, but they ignored him.

Indifference was a lot better than outright panic. Shrugging, he moved on.

The fourth kennel was the largest and it held the most. Seven puppies gamboled about. It was hard to tell what kind of breed mix they were. There seemed to be some German shepherd, along with maybe a splash of golden retriever, or something else he couldn't identify. The result was that the puppies looked somewhat wolfish, with narrow noses, yellow-gold eyes, and brown and tan markings on their soft, shaggy pelts.

As he watched, one puppy chewed its hind leg while one of its litter mates stalked up to it and pounced. Liam laughed as the pair fell over, growling at each other.

Bending over the gate, he reached down to pet one of the largest of the puppies. It promptly turned to gnaw on his fingers with needle-sharp teeth. Another, smaller puppy fixed on him and bounded to the gate. It scrabbled at the barrier.

The thing was, his parents hadn't been wrong. He really would have loved to have a puppy. But now he was going away to school, or at least he hoped he was.

If everything went well, he would be leaving behind everyone he knew. His mother and father. His new baby brother. He would be gambling everything to take a shot at a big unknown.

If everything didn't go well, and he didn't get into Glenhaven in time for the next term, he truly had no idea what he was going to do with himself.

He wished he had friends, because he could sure use a friend to talk to right now. But there was nobody. His last bunch of friends were years behind him in age and development. He had left them far behind with this latest growth spurt, and they wouldn't be looking at going to college for years.

He'd had a good talk with Hugh, but Hugh was like an uncle. Hugh could offer good advice, but he couldn't empathize with where Liam was at. Because nobody was where Liam was at. He was surrounded by people who loved him, yet he had never felt lonelier.

Everything felt at once too big and yet too restrictive. His chest constricted, and he couldn't breathe as the wide, wild world crushed down on him.

A woman bent over the gate beside him and held a long-fingered, tawny hand out to one of the puppies. She asked, "Which one are you going to pick?"

Liam paused, puzzled. He hadn't heard anyone come in through the glass door. He must have been more preoccupied with the puppies than he had realized.

"I'm just visiting with them," he said in a choked voice. "I can't actually have one."

"Of course you can have one." The woman scratched the puppy behind its ear, and it sat down, lifted its head to her and closed its eyes in bliss.

It was an odd thing to say to a total stranger. Liam gave her a sidelong, wary glance. The woman was dressed in a long black and gold tunic and black trousers, and thick gold bangles dangled at her wrists. As they both were leaning over the gate, he couldn't see much of her face, just a strong, high cheekbone and the graceful curve of her jaw.

It was hard to tell from such a position, but her body was long and muscled, and she looked as though she might be as tall as he was. Tawny hair curled down her back, as wild and untamed as a lion's mane.

"No, I really can't," he told her, leaning his elbows on the gate. "I might be going away to college soon."

"And you can't have a puppy while you're in college?"

Taken aback, he muttered, "Well, I—I guess I don't know. I hadn't really thought about it. I was sort of expecting that I might be staying in a dorm. If I get to go at all. Right now, my whole life feels like a blank page."

The woman picked up the puppy she had been petting. It wriggled happily in her hands, and she kissed its nose. "If your life is a blank page, that only means you have room to write your story. You have the power to tell that story the way you want to. I agree, staying in a dorm wouldn't be possible with a puppy. But if you stayed in an apartment, you could have one—that is, if you really wanted one. After all, young Cuelebre, it isn't as though your family can't afford to put you up in an apartment."

The walls seemed to reverberate with her words.

Young Cuelebre, she had said. Somehow this strange woman knew who he was. His hackles rose. Compulsively he scanned her for magic, or any other hint of Power.

There was nothing. Sucking in a breath, he tried to catch her scent.

All he could smell was the overwhelming, earthy smell of puppies that were too young to be housebroken.

Staring at the stranger's profile, he whispered, "How do you know to say that name?"

Chapter Five

THE WOMAN DIDN'T turn to face him. He watched the corner of her full mouth lift into a smile as the puppy in her cradling hands curled into a ball and fell asleep. "Everyone knows that name, young Cuelebre. Isn't that why you are willing to travel halfway across the world to get away from it?"

He hissed, "*Who are you?*"

"That doesn't matter," she said, dismissing his question with a shrug. "All that really matters is that everything does depend on what you want. If you want a puppy badly enough, you'll do whatever it takes to have one, and you'll fight to keep it."

As she spoke, he looked around wildly for any clues as to her identity. His gaze fell to the border of her tunic. Lions were embroidered along the bottom.

His pulse pounded in his ears. Slowly, he said, "You're wearing lions. Inanna, the goddess of Love, always has lions."

"Fitting, don't you think?" She stroked the puppy's forehead with a long, tapered forefinger. "So many people think love is an emotion. I love you, they say, and that is supposed to excuse all their bad behaviors and elevate them to a higher level just because they happen to feel something. That isn't love; it's an excuse. Love is like a lion. It's fierce and strong. It conquers fear and uncertainties, and it knows how to fight. Love fights to win and keep its mate, to do the right thing, to give to others in service, no matter what the cost. 'Greater love has no one than this: to lay down one's life for one's friends.'"

The scene blurred as tears filled Liam's eyes. He swiped at his nose. "That sounds like a quote."

"It is a quote," said the woman. "It's attributed to the man whose birthday is celebrated all over the world every December. Your sentinel Constantine knew of it. That man might have been a mess, but he knew how to love."

He whispered, "It also leaves a hole behind when they go."

"Yes, it does, and that is when you know you had something worth having." The woman turned to him. "If you really want a puppy, I think you should pick this one. She isn't the biggest in the litter, but she'll grow to be a strong, fine dog. Her life will be much too short, and you'll grieve when she's gone, but while she lives that life, she will stand by you through all your uncertainties. She'll comfort you when you are alone, even when you journey to a distant, strange place, and she'll guard your back when you need protection. And she will love you with all of her loyal, fierce heart. That, young

Cuelebre, is a worthy companion to have."

"But what if I take her, and the college won't let me keep her?" he asked.

Anxiously, he thought, what if the college won't take me in time?

Through the blur of his tears, he saw the woman smile.

"This is where you have a little faith that things will work out all right," she said. She offered the sleeping puppy to him, and without thinking, he reached out to receive it. The small, delicate body filled his hands.

The puppy stirred at the disruption, and it tried to open its eyes, but it was too sleepy. Showing its tongue in a wide, pink-tipped yawn, it sniffed at the air then snuggled into his palms.

As he looked down at the soft, warm body he cradled, the constriction around his chest finally began to ease. Warmth stole in, and comfort.

Look at her little puppy head. And those little puppy ears. Gently, he rubbed one of her paws. She stretched out her short, stubby puppy legs with a sigh, and he lost his heart.

Blinking hard to clear his gaze, he lifted his head to get a better look at the woman.

She was gone. There wasn't anybody in the large room, except for him.

He trembled. "Okay, that was pretty weird," he whispered to the puppy as he cradled her against his chest. "She was probably just another oddball New

Yorker, right? Goddesses don't talk to guys just because they're having some kind of internal meltdown. Right?"

The glass door swung open, and he spun around to face it.

Pia and the older woman walked into the room, and both were smiling.

"How did it go?" he asked his mom.

"For a first meeting, it went really well," she said. She turned to the other woman. "Eileen, thank you for taking the time to meet with me on Christmas Eve."

"It was entirely my pleasure, Lady Cuelebre," Eileen said as she held out her hand to shake. "Again, on behalf of the shelter, I can't thank you enough. I'll set up a time for the board to meet as soon after the New Year as I can."

"And in the meantime," Pia said with a pointed glance at Liam, "there will be no more animals euthanized unless medically you have no other option."

"Absolutely. We're still overcrowded, but with your very generous donation, we'll be able to hire new staff and buy enough supplies to care for all the animals we do have."

"Very good." Pia smiled.

The other woman gave Liam a curious glance, but other than that, she didn't comment on his presence. "Well, if you'll excuse me, I have a lot to attend to before we close this evening."

"Please, go do what you need to do," Pia told her. "I can see myself out."

"Merry Christmas," Eileen said, smiling at both of them.

"Merry Christmas," Pia and Liam replied together.

As soon as the other woman walked out of the room, Pia turned to look at Liam and the puppy.

"Your father texted to say he couldn't get free, but he's definitely going to be done by this evening, and he's taking tomorrow off so that we can travel back home. We've got to get ready for Isalynn Lefevre's niece to visit from the witches demesne in mid January. Then our part in that damn diplomatic pact made in DC two months ago will be done." Her smile turned indulgent. "That puppy is so darn cute, I can hardly stand it. She looks like a baby wolf, but I can't imagine the shelter would have let wolf mixed breeds be available for general adoption."

Liam listened with only half his attention. 'Have a little faith', the strange woman who was probably not a goddess had said. Still, it was good advice.

He bent his head over the sleeping puppy. "I want her."

"Aw." Pia's voice softened sympathetically. "It's hard to let go when puppy lust takes hold, isn't it?"

"No, you don't understand," Liam said, looking up at his mom. "I really want her."

Pia's expression changed. "But honey—you're going to college. Aren't you? You were so adamant about Glenhaven yesterday."

"Oh, I'm still going if they'll have me." Smiling down

at the dog, he stroked her small back. "I want to take the puppy with me. It will mean I can't stay in any dorms.... But you know, after thinking about it, I don't think I want to stay in a dorm anyway. I'm going to have to be on guard all the time about who I am and what my Wyr form is, and I think I really need to have a space where I can have some privacy to unwind." He added, "That is, if I can get in for the next term."

He was trying to have a little faith, but at the moment, that didn't take away any of his uncertainty.

Shifting her weight back onto one foot, Pia tilted her jaw as she thought about it. "You make a really good point about needing privacy," she said slowly. "I don't think any of us had gotten that far in our thinking yesterday. And I like the idea of you having a pet with you. It's really hard for me to think about you being off at school alone and cut off from us."

"There, you see," he crooned at his puppy.

"But Liam, she's going to be a lot of work. You'll have to potty train her, make sure she gets all her shots, and she will restrict your social life. You'll always be running home to let her out at lunchtime, and you might not get a full night's sleep for a couple of months. And there's other training to consider. By the size of those paws, she's going to grow up to be a big dog. You'll need to make sure she's well behaved."

"I don't need a lot of sleep," he told her. Bending farther, he pressed a kiss to the puppy's soft, furry head. "And I'll potty train her, and train her to be good, and

I'll spend lunchtimes with her too. I want her badly enough, I'll do whatever I have to in order to keep her. Okay?"

His mom took a deep breath. "Well," she said. "I think that's all any of us could ask you to do. As long as you're sure."

"I'm sure." He grinned at her.

She grinned back at him. "Holy smokes, my son is going off to college, and I'm only twenty six years old."

"Well, we *think* so," he stressed. "I *hope* so."

"*Pfft!*" She waved that aside. "And you're getting a dog too! Oh my God, we have so much stuff we need to buy. And we need to buy it right now, before the stores close for the night. What does a baby dog need? I have no idea."

"A bed, and a crate, and chew toys, and a collar and leash," he said. "Really good dog food. The best."

She stared at him. "She's going to piddle everywhere, and the penthouse is seventy-nine floors away from ground level. How do people have puppies in high-rise apartments? Somehow, they do."

While she spoke, the glass door opened again, and Eva strolled through. The other woman took one look at the puppy snoring in Liam's arms and started to laugh.

"You know what to do for living with a puppy in a high-rise apartment, don't you?" Liam asked her, giving his best coaxing smile.

Eva snorted. "Are you joking? You're not, are you? You're really going to adopt that dog? Okay, well, as long as you're staying in the penthouse, you're going to want pee pads and a grass litter box that you can set up on the balcony. There's plenty of room out there, so you can even tuck it out of sight if you want."

"A grass litter box?" Pia said cautiously.

"It's a square of real turf or artificial turf in a big fancy box with a sprinkler system and a drainage option," Eva told her. She paused. "Since it's the dead of winter right now, you'll obviously want to get the artificial turf."

Liam turned to his mom. "Do we need to get that if we're going home tomorrow anyway?"

"Yes," she said firmly. "You never know when we might need to come back to the city, and as long as you have that puppy, it will be good to have on hand."

"Perfect," Liam said with satisfaction. Happiness buoyed his spirits so that he laughed with joy.

"What are you going to name her?" Eva asked with a grin.

"I haven't decided yet." The puppy lay like a dead weight in his arms, her body lax in complete trust. "I was thinking of naming her Marika, or maybe Rika for short."

Pia raised her eyebrows. "After that little Dark Fae girl you went to school with in first grade?"

"Yup." He rubbed the puppy's round belly. "I have a feeling she's going to be just as fierce as Marika was."

"I like it," Pia declared. "It's a good name. Come on, we've got a lot to do. Let's get you through the adoption process, so we can pick up everything we need."

Liam reminded her, "You'll have to adopt her. Officially, I mean. Liam's too young, remember?"

Pia threw up her hands. *"Oy vey."*

LATER THAT EVENING, everything was done. All the supplies had been bought and delivered, and Liam had even set up the fancy grass litter box out on the balcony.

Eva had been right. There was plenty of room for Liam to tuck the large litter box out of sight, at least from the living room, and also against one of the concrete support pylons so that it was somewhat sheltered from the winter wind.

He was sprawled on the floor, playing tug of war with Rika while Pia cooked dinner, when his dad strode into the penthouse.

When Dragos laid eyes on Liam and the puppy, he stopped dead. His entrance got Rika's attention. The puppy turned to consider him, head cocked.

Then with a playful bark, she bounced across the room to attack one of Dragos's shoes.

Dragos cocked his head and gave Liam such an expressive look, he burst out laughing. "Mom!" he shouted. "Did you by any chance forget to tell Dad that we were bringing a puppy home?"

Something clattered in the kitchen. Pia said, "Damn it. Yes."

"Stop it," Dragos told the dog.

Growling, Rika tugged at his shoelace then sat to chew on one end. Bending, Dragos picked her up by the scruff of the neck and lifted her until she was at eye level. He told the puppy, "I said stop."

In answer, she yipped and wriggled, and tried to bite at his fingers.

Dragos carried her over to Liam and deposited her in his lap. "I'm sure there is a perfectly reasonable story attached to this."

"Absolutely," Liam said.

"And what about Glenhaven?" Dragos asked, one eyebrow up.

"I'm going to take her with me—if I get in. I guess we'll know one way or another, soon enough." He stroked Rika then set her on the floor. She promptly ran over to Dragos to bite at his shoelace again. Laughing, Liam lunged after her to scoop her up. "Sorry. I'll take her out."

"I'll just go make sure all the closet doors are closed." Dragos strode down the hall.

Liam carried Rika out onto the balcony and set her on the fake turf in the litter box. With a gigantic effort, she jumped off the box and raced around the balcony. He went after her and set her on the litter box. Happily she jumped off again. She loved the litter box game.

Somehow, it would all work out, he told himself for the thousandth time.

If he got into Glenhaven.

Realistically, it might take weeks before he knew anything. Waiting to hear one way or another was going to kill him.

His phone rang in his jeans pocket. Digging it out while he set Rika on the litter box again, he checked the number. The call wasn't from any number he recognized. He thumbed the answer button and said, "Hello?"

"Good evening, is this Liam Giovanni?" a pleasant male voice asked.

In a Scottish accent.

Surprise pounded in his ears. Clearing his throat, he replied, "Yes, it is. Who's calling?"

"My name is Ian Killian. I'm a representative of Glenhaven College. Is this a good time to talk?"

"Sure," he said. "I wasn't expecting to hear from you. At least, I mean, not so quickly, and it's Christmas Eve."

"Ach, Christmas Eve," Killian said in a tone that clearly dismissed such human things. "I had traveled to New York for the Masque, and I was about to leave for home again when I received an email from the dean with your application attached. I know this is short notice, but my flight leaves for Edinburgh tomorrow evening— would you by any chance have time to meet in person in the morning?"

"A-absolutely," he stuttered, while he fist pumped and leaped into the air, making Rika fall over from surprise. She bounded to her feet and barked at him.

"When and where would you like to meet?" Killian asked briskly.

Cupping his phone to shield the microphone from the puppy's barking, he tried to think. "Since tomorrow's

Christmas, there's actually not going to be much open," he said slowly. Dare he suggest it? "How about the Starbucks in Cuelebre Tower? The Tower is centrally located, and that Starbucks never closes."

"A sensible suggestion," Killian told him. "Let's say nine o'clock? It shouldna take long, just a half an hour or so."

"Sure," he said. "That would be great. Thank you."

"All right, I'll see you then."

Quickly, before the older male could hang up, Liam said, "Wait—Do you mind me asking what to expect tomorrow?"

"Not at all," Killian replied. "Your application looks quite impressive, young man. I'll just be wanting to verify some of the details. Perhaps you can show me a touch of your talents. If everything looks to be in order, I'll be submitting your request for a scholarship to the finance committee."

That sounded like it could be a lengthy process. He frowned. "How long will that take?"

"Scholarship students are fully funded, which is an expensive process, so the committee might not approve your application for another six months to a year."

His lips tightened. Rika was starting to shiver, so he scooped her up and tucked her inside his sweater, where she snuggled against his chest and promptly fell asleep.

He said, "What if I told you I've come up with financing on my own, so I won't be needing a scholarship after all?"

"Ach, well, that changes things completely," Killian said.

"Do you think my application might be approved in time for me to start the next term? I mean, if there's room for Glenhaven to take me."

"Young man, I can approve your application when I meet you tomorrow. As long as everything is in order, of course. And yes, there's room for you to start this next term, if you can be ready by then, and you don't mind being flexible on what kind of housing you get. If your financing is enough to allow you to get your own apartment, you should be fine. The new term begins on January fifteenth, so that isn't much time for you to prepare. But we can talk all about that tomorrow morning, so be sure to come with a list of your questions."

Excitement pounded through his body. He could hardly believe it, but it sounded like everything really would fall into place. "Yes—yes, I will. Thank you so much, Mr. Killian!"

"You're welcome, Mr. Giovanni. See you in the morning."

As Killian disconnected, Liam let out a loud whoop. Rika was sound asleep by that point and never stirred, but Dragos and Pia strode quickly into the living room, drawn by the noise.

He rushed inside and waved his phone at them. "That was a representative from Glenhaven College! He wants to meet me tomorrow morning!"

"You're kidding," Pia said faintly. "Already?"

"He said he came to New York for the Masque, so he's already here. The dean forwarded my application to him, and his flight leaves tomorrow evening, so we're meeting in the morning! The next term starts January fifteenth, so it's not quite as soon as I was afraid it would be. And if I can afford an apartment, he said there would be space for me!"

His dad and mom gave each other a long look. It was complicated, that look, filled with a lot of things Liam didn't know how to categorize. Wryness was there, and a touch of sadness, along with pride and acceptance.

"Kids these days," Dragos said quietly. "They grow up so fast."

"Supersonic fast," Pia said just as quietly. She laid a hand on her flat abdomen. "I guess we need to fasten our seat belts, because we're about to go through it all again."

It touched Liam's heart, how much they loved him. "Come on," he said gently. "Be happy for me."

Immediately, Pia strode over to throw her arms around him and hug him, puppy and all. "I am so happy for you," she told him. "And so proud of you, I don't know what to do with myself. I'm not going to lie to you, Liam—I just hate the thought of Glenhaven closing its doors for an entire term. But I understand why you need this, and I'm behind you every step of the way."

Dragos strode over and clapped him on the shoulder. "Good job. I'm proud of you too."

"Well," he felt compelled to say, "I'm not in quite

yet."

"Oh, for heaven's sake, *pfft*," Pia said, brushing his caution aside with a wave of her hand. "You're in."

"I think this calls for a toast," Dragos said. He looked into Liam's eyes with a smile. "How about a glass of champagne?"

Liam perked up. He wondered if he would like champagne. He knew he would like finding that out. "Hell yeah."

Pia's eyes sparkled. "Dinner's in the oven, so while we drink champagne and the puppy sleeps, I think we should open a few presents."

Liam nodded. "I second that idea."

While Dragos and Pia left to collect a chilled bottle of champagne and three flutes, Liam pulled Rika out from underneath his sweater and carefully settled her on her new dog bed. She was so sound asleep, she never noticed a thing.

"You need to crate her tonight," Pia said as she came back into the room carrying the champagne flutes. "She needs to get used to sleeping in her own bed, even if she cries a bit at first."

He nodded. Probably so. But he had a feeling he would let her out of the crate and let her sleep with him.

Dragos strolled back into the room, a bottle of champagne in one hand. Pia and Liam watched as he opened it and poured the frothing golden drink into the flutes. When he was done, Pia handed the flutes around, and then she raised hers in the air.

"To family," she said. "We can get through anything together. Even arguments and really weird stuff. Merry Christmas, guys. I love you with all my heart."

They clinked glasses, and Liam tasted champagne for the first time. He said, "Oh God. Oh damn."

Dragos and Pia laughed, and Dragos asked, "Is that good or bad?"

"It's very, very good." He took another sip and savored the flavor. He said fervently, "I love taste buds."

Dragos held his flute up for another toast. As Pia and Liam joined him, he looked at Liam and smiled.

Dragos said, "To your future, son. May it always be bright, and may you find your way home again when you're ready."

They clinked glasses again. Thinking of the golden woman, Liam asked, "Even if it is filled with really weird stuff?"

His parents laughed.

"Even then," Dragos replied.

Pia had the final word on that toast, as she added, "Especially then."

Happy Holidays
Love, Thea

Thank you!

Dear Readers,

Thank you for reading my short story, *Liam Takes Manhattan*. Dragos, Pia and Liam Cuelebre are some of my favorite characters, and I'm delighted to share this new story with you. I hope you have as much fun visiting with them as I did!

Would you like to stay in touch and hear about new releases? You can:

- Sign up for my newsletter at: www.theaharrison.com
- Follow me on Twitter at @TheaHarrison
- Like my Facebook page at facebook.com/TheaHarrison

Reviews help other readers find the books they like to read. I appreciate each and every review, whether positive or negative.

Liam Takes Manhattan is the final story in a three-story arc featuring Dragos, Pia and their son Liam. The first is *Dragos Goes to Washington*, and the second is *Pia Does Hollywood*. While each story is written so that it can be enjoyed individually, the reading experience will be stronger if you enjoy all three in order.

Happy reading!
Thea

Pia Does Hollywood

After making a diplomatic pact with humankind and the other leaders of the Elder Races, Pia Cuelebre, mate to Dragos Cuelebre, Lord of the Wyr, reluctantly heads to Hollywood to spend a week with the Light Fae Queen, Tatiana, before the busy Masque season hits New York in December.

Dragos has never let the lack of an invitation stop him from doing anything he wanted. Unwilling to let his mate make the trip without him, he travels to southern California in secret to be with her.

But when an ancient enemy launches a shattering assault against the Light Fae, Dragos and Pia must intercede. The destruction threatens to spread and strike a mortal blow against all of the magically gifted, both human and Elder Race alike.

Working with the Light Fae to neutralize the danger, Dragos and Pia find their deepest vulnerabilities challenged and their most closely held secrets threatened with exposure.

Pia Does Hollywood is the second part of a three-story series about Pia, Dragos, and and their son, Liam. Each story stands alone, but fans might want to read all three: *Dragos Goes to Washington*, *Pia Does Hollywood*, and *Liam Takes Manhattan*.

Look for these titles from Thea Harrison

CPSIA information can be obtained
at www.ICGtesting.com
Printed in the USA
LVOW13s1518200118
563310LV00012B/700/P